Vampire Kisses

BLOOD RELATIUES

VOLUME II

Ellen Schreiber
Art by rem

HAMBURG // LONDON // LOS ANGELES // TOKYO

KATHERINE TEGEN BOOKS
An Imprint of HarperCollinsPublishers

Vampire Kisses: Blood Relatives Vol. 2
By Ellen Schreiber
Art by rem (Priscilla Hamby)
Adapted by Diana McKeon Charkalis

Editors - Alexis Kirsch, Julie Lansky
Associate Editor - Katherine Schilling
Lettering - Mike Estacio
Toning & Inking - Elisa Kwon
Cover Design - Jennifer Carbajal
Digital Imaging Manager - Chris Buford
Pre-Production Supervisor - Vince Rivera
Production Manager - Lucas Rivera
Managing Editor - Vy Nguyen
Creative Director - Al-Insan Lashley
Editor-in-Chief - Rob Tokar
Publisher - Mike Kiley
President and C.O.O. - John Parker
C.E.O. and Chief Creative Officer - Stu Levy

A ⊙ TOKYOPOP Manga

TOKYOPOP and ⊙ are trademarks or registered trademarks of TOKYOPOP Inc.

TOKYOPOP Inc.
5900 Wilshire Blvd., Suite 2000
Los Angeles, CA 90036

E-mail: info@TOKYOPOP.com
Come visit us online at www.TOKYOPOP.com

For information address HarperCollins Children's Books, a division of HarperCollins Publishers,
1350 Avenue of the Americas, New York, NY 10019.
www.harperteen.com

Library of Congress catalog card number: 2008930198
ISBN 978-0-06-134082-6

1 2 3 4 5 6 7 8 9 10
❖
First Edition

CONTENTS

Welcome to DULLSVILLE

MEET RAVEN MADISON: SPORTING BLACK LIPSTICK, BLACK NAIL POLISH, AND A SHARP WIT, RAVEN IS AN OUTSIDER AT CONSERVATIVE DULLSVILLE HIGH. CURIOUS AND FEARLESS, SHE'S NOT AFRAID TO TAKE ON ANYONE, FROM GOSSIPING GIRLS TO EVEN SCARIER, NEFARIOUS CREATURES OF THE NIGHT. AMAZINGLY, RAVEN'S GREATEST WISH HAS COME TRUE—SHE'S DATING A REAL VAMPIRE. THE ONLY PROBLEM IS THAT SHE HAS TO WAIT UNTIL SUNDOWN TO SEE HIM AND MUST KEEP HIS TRUE IDENTITY A SECRET.

MEET ALEXANDER STERLING:
HANDSOME AND ELUSIVE, ALEXANDER IS THE TEEN VAMPIRE OF RAVEN'S DREAMS. HE LIVES IN A MANSION ON TOP OF BENSON HILL, AND ONLY EMERGES AT NIGHT. A SENSITIVE ARTIST, THIS PALE PRINCE OF DARKNESS HAS SOULFUL EYES AND A HEART TO MATCH. HE IS WITTY WITH A MACABRE SENSE OF HUMOR, BUT KIND AND GENTLE WHEN IT COMES TO RAVEN. WHEN RAVEN FINDS HERSELF IN TROUBLE, HE'S THE FIRST ONE TO SPRING TO HER DEFENSE.

MEET BECKY MILLER:
RAVEN'S ONLY GIRLFRIEND, BECKY IS MORE SHY AND RESERVED THAN HER GOTHIC COUNTERPART. SINCE MEETING IN THE THIRD GRADE, RAVEN HAS BEEN BECKY'S BEST FRIEND AND BODYGUARD, PROTECTING HER FROM NAME CALLING AND PLAYGROUND CLASHES. BECKY OFTEN FINDS HERSELF EMBROILED IN RAVEN'S MISADVENTURES, BUT THESE DAYS SHE HAS SOME EXCITEMENT OF HER OWN. SHE'S HEAD OVER HEELS IN LOVE WITH MATT WELLS, A POPULAR BUT GOOD-HEARTED GUY AT SCHOOL WHOM SHE'S STARTED DATING.

MEET CLAUDE STERLING: CLAUDE IS ALEXANDER'S HOT AND OFTEN HOTHEADED HALF-VAMPIRE COUSIN. COMPETITIVE SINCE BIRTH, CLAUDE HAS ONE THING ON HIS MIND—BECOMING A FULL VAMPIRE. CLAUDE HAS BROUGHT HIS GANG WITH HIM FROM ROMANIA TO DULLSVILLE TO RETRIEVE MUCH NEEDED VIALS OF PURE VAMPIRE BLOOD HIS GRANDMOTHER HAD HIDDEN. DRINKING THESE VIALS IS THE ONLY WAY THEY CAN BE TURNED. AND SINCE ALEXANDER WON'T GIVE THE VIALS UP, CLAUDE THINKS RAVEN IS HIS TICKET TO UNEARTHING THEIR LOCATION.

MEET KAT: SULTRY AND DECEPTIVE, KAT IS CLAUDE'S RIGHT-HAND GIRL. SHE USES HER CATLIKE BEGUILES TO CREATE A WEDGE BETWEEN RAVEN AND ALEXANDER. THOUGH SHE'S OFTEN FOUND FILING HER NAILS, SHE'S ONE TOUGH COOKIE AND HATES PLAYING BACKSEAT WHEN PLANS ARE BEING MADE.

MEET ROCCO: THE MUSCLE OF CLAUDE'S GANG, ROCCO WOULD RATHER BE THROWING PUNCHES THAN USING BRAINPOWER TO GET HIS HANDS ON THE VIALS. AND WHILE HE'S JUST AS HUNGRY AS THE OTHERS FOR THE VIALS, ROCCO USUALLY LETS CLAUDE LEAD THE WAY—EVEN IF IT MIGHT BE THE WRONG DIRECTION.

MEET TRIPP: THE BRAINS IN CLAUDE'S GANG, TRIPP CONTRIBUTES HIS TECHNO-SAVVY SKILLS TO HELP THE GANG WHEN NEEDED. NOT ONE WITH MUCH BRAWN, TRIPP IS USUALLY THE FIRST TO HIDE BEHIND ROCCO WHEN DANGER LOOMS NEAR.

MEET TREVOR: RAVEN'S KHAKI-CLAD NEMESIS, TREVOR IS GORGEOUS, RICH, AND A SUPER-JOCK. SO WHAT'S NOT TO LIKE? HIS PERSONALITY. SINCE KINDERGARTEN, TREVOR'S BEEN BENT ON MAKING LIFE MISERABLE FOR RAVEN. HE'D NEVER ADMIT IT, BUT HE'S MORE ATTRACTED TO HER THAN REPULSED AND HAS HAD A CRUSH ON HER SINCE THEY WERE KIDS. WHEN TREVOR'S NOT DOMINATING THE SOCCER FIELD, HE'S USUALLY STARTING RUMORS OR PESTERING RAVEN, HIS "MONSTER GIRL."

CHAPTER 5: CLUELESS IN DULLSVILLE

AKHOO

THIS SHOULD WARD OFF THOSE VINDICTIVE VAMPIRES, AT LEAST FOR A LITTLE WHILE.

GIVE THAT TO ME AT ONCE!

BUT GRAND-MOTHER, I WAS JUST CURIOUS.

SILENCE! NOT ANOTHER WORD.

YOU TWO WOULD DO WELL TO REMEMBER WHAT CURIOSITY DID TO THE CAT.

NOW GO TO YOUR ROOMS AT ONCE. I AM VERY DISAP-POINTED IN YOU BOTH.

WHAT ARE YOU DOING UP? IT'S LATE.

I WANT TO TAKE ANOTHER LOOK AT THAT MAP.

SO GO. WHAT DO YOU WANT WITH ME?

C'MON. THERE MUST BE A PRETTY BIG SECRET IN IT OR GRANDMOTHER WOULDN'T HAVE BEEN SO ANGRY.

Don't you want to check it out?

GRAND-MOTHER SAID TO LEAVE IT ALONE.

OH, YOU'RE ALWAYS SUCH A GOOD BOY. ARE YOU AFRAID TO DISOBEY GRANDMOTHER?

!

DON'T WORRY, EVERYTHING WILL BE ALL RIGHT.

MR. PERKINS?

BLOOD DRIVE

I'D LIKE TO VOLUNTEER TO HELP WITH THE SCHOOL BLOOD DRIVE.

HOW DID YOU SLEEP, DEAR?

GREAT-- DEAD TO THE WORLD.

THE SOONER YOU GET THAT MAP, THE SOONER YOU CAN BE LIKE US.

DON'T YOU NOTICE HOW EVERYONE STARES WHENEVER WE WALK INTO A ROOM?

BUT NOW I'M STARTING TO SEE THAT LIVING AS ONE OF THE UNDEAD IS JUST NOT AS GLAMOROUS AS I THOUGHT.

THEY'RE TOTALLY CLUELESS. I MEAN, KAT CAN'T EVEN TELL IF SHE'S HAVING A BAD HAIR DAY.

AND SHE ALWAYS HAS TO BE ON GUARD.

?

ZIP

WHAT'S THE DEAL, FREAK?

YOU LOOK BEAUTIFUL.

THE CANDLELIGHT REALLY SHOWS OFF YOUR GHOSTLY PALLOR.

THANK YOU. I USE SPF 400.

IT SHOWS. SO YOU SAID THERE WAS SOMETHING YOU WANTED TO TALK ABOUT?

YEAH.

I CAN'T STOP WONDERING WHAT HAPPENED TO THE REAL MAP AND THE REAL VIALS THAT YOUR GRAND-MOTHER HID.

THERE AREN'T ANY CLUES AT ALL IN YOUR GRAND-MOTHER'S ROOM?

RAVEN! ELVIS OR THE BEATLES?

HOW ABOUT CRUX-SHADOWS?

UHHH...

THEY HAVE. BOBBY DARIN.

HEY, THEY'VE GOT THE STONES. REMEMBER WHEN WE DANCED TO THEM AT THE PROM?

How's that?

BUT PROMISE ME, IF ONE OF THEM EVEN STEPS ONE FOOT NEAR YOU, YOU'LL LET ME KNOW.

DUH! AND I'LL CALL 911.

PERFECT.

BECKY, LET'S CHOOSE SOME DESSERT!

ANYTHING WITH CHOCOLATE!

MIND IF WE CRASH YOUR PARTY?

!

LOOKS LIKE I DON'T HAVE A CHOICE. WHAT DO YOU WANT?

MAYBE I WON'T NEED YOUR HELP AFTER ALL. I HAVE OTHER WAYS OF GETTING THAT MAP.

EVEN FULL-BLOODED VAMPIRES LIKE YOUR BELOVED ALEXANDER HAVE TO SLEEP SOMETIME...AND ONCE HE'S INSIDE THAT COFFIN HE'LL NEVER SEE ME COMING...

THIS GUY IS A MENACE. I CAN'T LET HIM HURT ALEXANDER OR JAMESON.

I CAN ONLY IMAGINE WHAT HE HAS IN MIND.

OHHHH... MY NOSE...

NICE BLOCK, BRO. WALK IT OFF...

HMPH.

OW...

ALL RIGHT! WAY TO GO, GUYS!

RAVEN! WAIT UNTIL THEY SCORE A GOAL!

Hmph.

Oh...

KWAK

Ooh!

THOSE ARE KIND OF AWESOME.

ALEXANDER GAVE THEM TO ME.

BIOLOGY 101

DRACULA

THEY'RE CALLED BLACK BEAUTIES AND THEY WERE SHIPPED FROM ROMANIA.

THEY SAY THEY'RE DYED WITH THE BLOOD OF VAMPIRE BATS.

Ewwww!

TOTALLY GROSS.

HEY, ANGEL.

ARE YOU AVOIDING ME?

EVERY CHANCE I GET.

TAKE YOUR HANDS OFF ME.

YOUR LIPS SAY NO, BUT THE CHEMISTRY BETWEEN US SAYS YES.

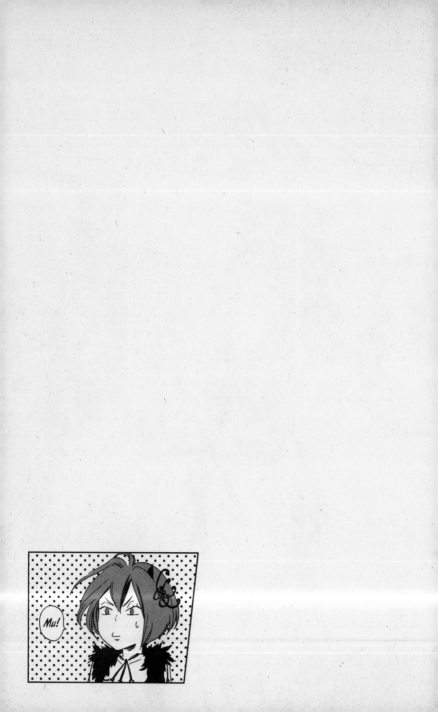

AT LAST! I'M FREEZING OUT HERE.

I'LL TAKE CARE OF THAT.

ANY SIGN OF MY COUSIN AND HIS LACKEYS?

NO, AND I'VE BEEN KEEPING WATCH. WHAT IF THEY DON'T SHOW UP?

GRAB

...

STOP! YOU'LL WAKE UP THE WHOLE NEIGHBOR-HOOD.

Huff!

Huff!

DARN, EVEN VAMPIRE DUDES WON'T ASK FOR DIRECTIONS WHEN THEY CAN'T FIGURE OUT A MAP.

PFFT!

IT'S LIKE THE THREE STOOGES MEETS BRIDE OF DRACULA.

HEY !!

DASH

SWSH

SWSH

FWOOOSH

BAM

I'M SORRY, CLAUDE. YOU STILL DON'T HAVE...

...THE SELF-CONTROL IT TAKES TO WIELD THE POWER THAT THESE VIALS POSSESS.

CAN YOU
BELIEVE
IT?!!

HE'S CRAZY WITH POWER AND YOU DON'T EVEN KNOW IT.

THAT'S NOT TRUE.

REAL-LY?

WHAT IF I OFFERED TO TAKE YOU TO ROMANIA?

HE'D NEVER ALLOW IT.

HE WANTS TO TRAP YOU HERE IN DULLSVILLE.

AND WHY ON EARTH WOULD I WANT TO GO WITH *YOU?*

HI THERE.

DON'T DO THAT...

YOU SCARED ME!!

My

TO BE CONTINUED...

BONUS STRIPS

COMING SOON . . .
VAMPIRE KISSES: BLOOD RELATIVES 3

With Alexander's ominous cousin Claude and his gritty gang still roaming Dullsville, Raven and her hot vampire beau have more to worry about than their nocturnal-only romance. And now that Claude knows he's been tricked out of the blood-filled vials that could turn him and his gang into full vampires, the couple must be extra cautious. Anything's possible when it comes to Claude, and Raven's family could be in mortal danger. When Claude strangely buddies up with Raven's own nemesis, Trevor, invitations soon go out for a mysterious party. This isn't your average high school party. Could Claude be scheming to turn Dullsville High into Vampire High? But the joke might be on Alexander and Raven this time. They must try to stop the fierce foursome from finding the real map and vials, and also question what's most at stake in the end...

Vampire Kisses
BLOOD RELATIVES

FROM NOVEL TO MANGA

The Making of Vampire Kisses: Blood Relatives

WELCOME TO THE SECOND BEHIND-THE-SCENES
LOOK AT THE MAKING OF THE *VAMPIRE KISSES* MANGA!
VOLUME 2 FEATURES TONS OF NEW CHARACTERS AND HOT
OUTFITS THAT WILL MAKE MY CLOSET TOTALLY JEALOUS!
AND CHECK OUT SOME CLOTHING DESIGNS THAT RAVEN
NEVER EVEN GOT TO WEAR IN THE ACTUAL MANGA!
—ELLEN SCHREIBER

RAVEN'S FASHION

FOR CASUAL OR SCHOOL WEAR, RAVEN KNOWS HOW TO ROCK THE GOTH
LOOK WITH A HINT OF PUNK. WHAT'S HER SIGNATURE PIECE IN THE MANGA?
ARM-WARMERS! AND REM'S KNOWLEDGE OF THE LATEST TRENDS ADDS SOME
EYE CANDY TO THE MANGA WHEN IT COMES TO RAVEN'S CLOTHES. NOW I
JUST NEED TO FIND OUT WHERE TO GET ONE OF THOSE CUTE BAT BAGS!

RAVEN KNOWS HOW TO MIX GOTH INTO ANY OCCASION—JUST CHECK HER OUT ON THE LEFT! THIS DRESS AND CORSET OUTFIT WAS THE FIRST DESIGN CREATED FOR THE FLOWER CONSERVATORY DATE SCENE IN THE BOOK. THOUGH RAVEN LOOKS SMASHING IN A BLACK DRESS WITH WHITE CORSET, I THOUGHT IT MIGHT BE TOO MUCH, SO WE WENT WITH A SIMPLER DESIGN IN THE END.

White corsette →

Mom and Dad

EVEN THOUGH THEY ONLY APPEAR BRIEFLY, I WANTED TO MAKE SURE RAVEN'S
FAMILY MADE A CAMEO IN VOLUME 2. I LOVED THE DESIGN FOR RAVEN'S
MOM IMMEDIATELY! SHE WAS EXACTLY AS I ALWAYS PICTURED HER! FOR
RAVEN'S DAD, I WAS UNSURE ABOUT JUST HOW "ROUND" HE SHOULD BE. THE
FINAL VERSION MAY HAVE ENDED UP BEING A LITTLE MORE MUSCULAR THAN I
HAD IMAGINED HIM, BUT THEN AGAIN, HE DOES PLAY A LOT OF GOLF..

HENRY AND BILLY

AND DON'T FORGET WHAT EVERY GIRL PROTAGONIST CAN'T DO WITHOUT—A LITTLE BROTHER TO PICK ON! BILLY BOY NEEDED MORE LOVE SO I MADE SURE HE GOT SCREEN TIME IN VOLUME 2. (DID EVERYONE CATCH HIM IN VOLUME 1?!) REM'S DESIGN FOR HIM (ON THE RIGHT) WAS SPOT-ON FROM THE START. MAYBE SHE KNOWS A THING OR TWO ABOUT CUTE LITTLE BROTHERS... HENRY (ON THE LEFT), HOWEVER, NEEDED SEVERAL REVISIONS BECAUSE REM WAS DRAWING HIM TOO CUTE. THE FINAL DESIGN SHOWS HIM IN ALL HIS NERDY GLORY!

TREVOR AND MATT

TREVOR

AS RAVEN'S HIGH SCHOOL NEMESIS IN THE NOVELS, TREVOR JUST HAD TO MAKE
AN APPEARANCE IN THE MANGA! REM CAPTURED HIS BAD-BOY ALLURE PERFECTLY.
BUT YOU'LL SEE THE FINAL VERSION ON THE LEFT WHERE WE MADE HIS HAIR JUST
A LITTLE LONGER. BECKY'S BEAU MATT WAS GREAT RIGHT OFF THE BAT. I LOVE
THE SCENE ON THE SOCCER FIELD WITH TREVOR AND ROCCO! LOOK FOR TREVOR
IN VOLUME 3 WHERE HE MAY HAVE A BIGGER ROLE...

JAMESON

REM WAS VERY INSPIRED WHEN DRAWING THE CREEPY YET SOMEHOW
ATTRACTIVE BUTLER OF THE STERLING FAMILY. I WAS FIRST PRESENTED
WITH TONS OF POSSIBLE DESIGNS FOR HIM—JUST LOOK AT THE
COLLAGE BELOW! THEY WERE ALL SO DIFFERENT!

HERE'S THE JAMESON DESIGN THAT WAS CHOSEN!

A FEW MORE DESIGNS LATER, AND WE'D FOUND THE RIGHT JAMESON! IT'S TOO BAD JAMESON ONLY APPEARS IN A FEW PAGES BECAUSE HE IS SUCH A COMBINATION OF CREEPY AND CUTE! I WILL HAVE TO FIND A WAY TO SNEAK HIM INTO VOLUME 3.

MORE FASHION

BECKY EXUDES CUTENESS IN A '60S JUMPER SKIRT WITH BULGING POCKETS. I'M GLAD SHE AND MATT GOT MORE ATTENTION THIS TIME AROUND. AND KAT REALLY GOT TO STRUT HER STUFF IN THIS VOLUME, WITH AN ARRAY OF NEW OUTFITS. I LOVE THE PEACOCK-INSPIRED OUTFIT SHE WORE AT THE FLOWER CONSERVATORY. VERY FLAPPERISH.

CLAUDE AND ALEXANDER

HERE ARE THE OUTFITS THESE TWO WEAR AT THE END OF THE VOLUME. COULD THEY GET ANY HOTTER? EVEN ROCCO CAN'T HELP BUT NOTICE. REM ALWAYS MAKES SURE TO INCLUDE NEW ACCESSORIES IN CLAUDE'S WARDROBE—HERE WE HAVE A ONE-OF-A-KIND SKELETON HANDPRINT T-SHIRT AND SNAKE ARMBAND. I NEED TO GET MY HANDS ON ALEXANDER'S SKULL VEST BUTTONS AND SPIDER BROOCH!!

Keep reading for more of Raven and
Alexander's juicy story in:

Vampire Kisses 5
The Coffin Club

1

Bat Out of Hell

I flew from class like a bat out of hell.

Dullsville High's bell rang its final year-end ring and I was the first student to arrive at my locker. Normally the sound of the bell grated on my nerves like a woodpecker hammering on a sycamore, but this time the buzzing was as melodious as the sound of a harpsichord. It signaled one thing: summer vacation.

The two words rolled off my tongue like the sweet-tasting nectar of the blossoming honeysuckles. Aren't all vacations sweet? Given. However, summer vacation beats out its sister vacations—spring and winter break. Summer vacation surpasses them all with its incomparable advantages—two and a half months of freedom from textbooks, teachers, and torment. No detentions, lectures, or pop quizzes. No more spending an eight-hour day in the confines of Dullsville High, being the only goth in the preppy-filled school, or trying to lift an overslept pre-caffeinated head off my wooden desk. And most important, I could sleep in late. Just like a vampire.

My red and white school-colored handcuffs had been slipped off my wrists.

I was so pumped I even beat model student and my best friend, Becky, to her locker. It was the last time I'd have to remember, or forget, as I often did, the lock's random coordinates. Unreturned textbooks, notebooks, candy wrappers, and CDs filled the tiny metal closet. Forever the procrastinator, I waited until the final moment to clean it out. Unlike other lockers that had actual photographs of couples, staring back at me were oil-based pictures of me and Alexander that he'd painted and surprised me with, by hanging them in my locker. I gazed at them adoringly and carefully untacked one when I became distracted by the huge mess in front of me. I figured I needed a wheelbarrow to haul the load to Becky's truck but instead dragged out a dented garbage can and tossed out anything that I hadn't paid for.

"Summer's here! Can you believe it?" Becky said,

catching up to me. We clasped hands and shrieked like we had just won tickets to a sold-out concert.

"It's finally here!" I exclaimed. "No more tardy slips or calls to my parents about dress codes."

Becky opened her locker, which had already been cleaned out. Photos of her and Matt presumably had been placed in a scrapbook with colorful captions, beautiful borders, and funky heart-shaped stickers. She examined the empty locker for anything else she might have forgotten.

"It looks like you even dusted it," I teased.

"This is going to be the best summer ever, Raven. This is the first summer we both will have boyfriends. To think, we'll be lying poolside with the hottest guys in Dullsville."

I spotted a painting of Alexander and me in front of Hatsy's Diner that still hung on the inside of my locker door. The stars twinkled above us and we were lit by the glow of the moon.

"Well, one of us will be," I said. And I wasn't referring to the fact that my boyfriend wouldn't be able to worship the sun.

I had a bigger problem—he wasn't even in Dullsville.

Becky must have read my wistful expression. "I bet Alexander will be back anytime now to have graveside picnics with you," Becky offered with a bright smile.

Alexander and his creepy-but-kind butler, Jameson, had driven the ailing tween vampire, Valentine Maxwell, to Hipsterville in hopes of reuniting him with his nefariously Draculine siblings, Jagger and Luna. After Valentine tried to sink his tiny fangs into my little brother, Billy Boy, my sibling and his best friend, Henry, began questioning his possible nocturnal identity. While Alexander was upstairs in his attic room saving the sickly boy with Jameson's Romanian concoctions, I figured out and confirmed Jagger's and Luna's location—the Coffin Club. And with that, Alexander was forced to leave me behind in Dullsville as he reunited Valentine with his older siblings. Alexander had promised me that he would return to Dullsville shortly. However, what we thought would be an overnight visit to Hipsterville turned into two, then three days. Then longer.

The sultry homeschooled Romanian vampire Alexander had brought life into my already darkened one. As the lonely old Mansion remained empty of its unearthly inhabitants, I began to miss specific things about him— the way he softly brushed my hair away from my face or traced the lace of my skirt with his ghost white fingers. I missed his dreamy chocolate brown eyes, his bright, sexy smile, his tender lips pressed to mine.

I managed to remove myself as the third wheel from Matt and Becky's go-cart of fun. In the moonlit evenings, instead of reluctantly cheering on the school's soccer team, I often visited the empty Mansion, sitting beneath its skeletal trees, by its wrought-iron gates, or on its uneven weed-filled cracked cement front steps. Other times, I'd hang out in the gazebo where Alexander and I'd shared romantic desserts and stolen kisses.

I assured myself that at any moment I'd see the headlights of Jameson's Mercedes beaming up the winding driveway, but every night I went home alone, the driveway devoid of any hearse-like vehicles.

I crossed each passing day off my Emily the Strange calendar with a giant black **X**. It was starting to look like a one-sided tic-tac-toe game. Occasionally the doorbell rang, and when it did, I'd race to the front door in wild expectation of Alexander wrapping his pale arms around me, scooping me up, and planting me with a passionate kiss. Instead of being greeted by my boyfriend, I was met by the Flower Power delivery woman holding a bouquet of roses. My already darkened bedroom was beginning to resemble Dullsville's funeral home.

With each passing day, I wondered what could be taking him so long. Was he once again protecting me from something dangerous and underworldly? My boyfriend, always shrouded in a bit of mystery, only made me love him more.

I had secured the painting of us in my backpack and then untacked a special item next to it—my Coffin Club barbed-wire bracelet.

The Coffin Club. The most gothically haunting nightspot in Hipsterville. I'd stumbled upon the hangout when I visited the funky town a few months ago. Unlike any other club I'd ever been to, the Coffin Club was the antithesis of Dullsville High. It was the first place where I really fit in, surrounded by similar taste, style, and attitude. I dreamed of returning there with Alexander on my arm. Only now I was miles away from my favorite nightclub and my favorite guy.

I untacked the painting of Alexander and me dancing at Dullsville's golf course.

I'd give anything to be rockin' with Alexander again. I imagined a painting that I could only fathom adding to my collection: one of Alexander and me dancing underneath the suspended deathly pale mannequins of the Coffin Club.

Just then Matt interrupted my daydream and gave Becky a peck on the neck—something I was desperately missing from Alexander.

Becky was right. I knew I'd see Alexander again—it

was just a matter of when. But I was growing restless.

"I'd have thought you would have had that cleaned out days ago," Matt said. "Do you need help?"

"Thanks, but I want to savor this moment. I'll meet you guys out front."

As my favorite couple headed outside, a group of girls clutching designer purses and shoes passed by me like they were strutting down a catwalk, talking about European trips and boarding-school-style camps they'd be attending.

I just looked forward to the one place I *wouldn't* have to go—Dullsville High.

The warm summer air breezed through the open classroom doors and windows. I felt a few inches taller. I slung my backpack over my shoulder and briskly walked past the open classrooms.

I was just a few feet away from freedom. I reached out to push the main door open when someone jumped in front of me.

Nothing could spoil my mood today—not on my favorite day of the year. Well, almost nothing. Trevor Mitchell, lifelong nemesis and khaki-wearing thorn in my side, was staring down at me. "You didn't think I'd let you leave without saying good-bye?"

"Step aside before my boots make contact with your

shins," I warned him.

"I haven't seen Monster Boy for weeks. Are you keeping him buried somewhere special?"

"Out of my way before I call the morgue. I think they have a vacancy."

"I'm really going to miss not seeing you every day." Trevor held his gaze a tad too long, like it had just hit him what he'd said. I could tell he was serious and it surprised him as much as it did me.

"I'm sure you'll get over it. You'll have your pick of über-tanned *Baywatch* beauties to keep you busy."

"But what will *you* do? I heard Monster Boy left town. Forever. That will leave you in town all summer alone."

I hated that a rumor had started about Alexander being gone.

"He hasn't left . . . forever," I defended. "He's coming back. But it really doesn't matter because I'm going to see him. We're spending the summer together out of town and away from *you*."

I knew I was fibbing, but the thought of Trevor hanging out with lifeguards on each arm and mocking me while I waited alone at the Mansion made my mortal blood boil.

Trevor wasn't thwarted by my challenge. It only spurred him on.

"Then how about one kiss?" he said with a sexy grin. "Something to remember me by?" Though I had hints from Valentine of Trevor's inner desire for me, I was still suspect. I never knew what was going on in Trevor's head, much less his heart. I wasn't even sure he had one. Trevor was gorgeous—there was no doubt about it. His green melt-worthy eyes and his chiseled face could easily make him the next *Sports Illustrated* cover boy. But I was never sure if Trevor really liked me or just liked bullying me. Either way, he didn't move out of my way and instead leaned into me. There was only one guy I was going to kiss and that was Alexander.

I pushed my hand to his chest.

Trevor leered at me with a sexy grin. The more I fought back, the more he liked it. I was Trevor's ultimate soccer opponent and he was always desperate for one more game.

I paused for a moment and gazed up at the guy who'd tormented me since kindergarten. Trevor was really the only person who paid attention to me at school, besides Becky. I wasn't sure I wouldn't miss seeing him every day, too.

"I'll give you something to remember *me* by," I said. "The back of my head."

I pushed past him and escaped through the door to freedom.

I stepped out of Dullsville High and into the bright glare of the sun.

The year was behind me. Overall, it had been the best year of my life, for I'd met, dated, danced, and fallen in love with Alexander Sterling.

Students were walking home or getting into their daddies' overpriced luxury cars, heading off to begin their months of fun in the sun with people just like them. I'd spent a whole school year surrounded by people like Trevor.

My nemesis really forced me into seeing the light. It was time for me to be with people of my own kind. I wasn't going to spend my summer sans Alexander, much less another day.

There was only one thing keeping me and Alexander apart now. Me.

And that could easily be fixed with just a phone call.

Sizzles in a manga debut!